TALES FROM
THE BROTHERS GRIMM

SELECTED AND ILLUSTRATED

BY LISBETH ZWERGER

minedition
North American edition published 2013 by Michael Neugebauer Publishing Ltd. Hong Kong

English translation copyright © 2012 by Anthea Bell
Illustrations copyright © 2012 by Lisbeth Zwerger
"The Seven Ravens" copyright © Nord-Sud Verlag AG, Zurich. Reprinted by kind permission.
Rights arranged with "minedition" Rights and Licensing AG, Zurich, Switzerland.
Michael Neugebauer Publishing Ltd., Unit 23, 7F, Kowloon Bay Industrial Centre, 15 Wang Hoi Road,
Kowloon Bay, Hong Kong. Phone +852 2147 0303, e-mail: info@minedition.com
This book was printed in July 2013 at L.Rex Printing Co Ltd 3/F., Blue Box Factory Building,
25 Hing Wo Street, Tin Wan, Aberdeen, Hong Kong, China
Typesetting in Carmina BT by Gudrun Zapf Hesse
Color separation by Fotolitho AG, Gossau, Switzerland
Library of Congress Cataloging-in-Publication Data available upon request.

ISBN 978-988-8240-53-1

10 9 8 7 6 5 4 3 2 1
First impression

For more information please visit our website: www.minedition.com

TALES FROM THE BROTHERS GRIMM

SELECTED
AND ILLUSTRATED BY
LISBETH ZWERGER
TRANSLATED
BY ANTHEA BELL

Tales of the oral tradition written down to last
The famous collection of the brothers Jacob and Wilhelm Grimm

The first edition of 86 tales collected by the Grimm brothers was published 200 years ago. It contained many of the tales that are still among the most popular: "Little Red Cap," "The Frog King," "Briar Rose," and others. Several more editions followed. Jacob and Wilhelm Grimm were linguistic scholars who also wrote a work on German Grammar and began to compile a German Dictionary. Both brothers supported the unification of the many separate German states, and were dismissed from their posts at the university of Göttingen because of their political opinions. They found a new place to live and work in Berlin, and their collections of fairy tales became the most popular of all their books. Since their own time, much light has been cast on the way they collected the tales. Readers imagined them travelling from place to place, writing down stories told by old peasant women. However, the two scholars' intention was, rather, to trace the course taken by the "wisdom of the people" back to its mythological sources. In this they were continuing the work of the Romantic poets Clemens Brentano and Achim von Arnim, in their famous folk-song collection *The Boy's Magic Horn*.

Jacob and Wilhelm Grimm set about collecting fairy tales in a very practical way. One of their most important informants was Dorothea Viehmann, not an old peasant but an educated woman of French descent. Her knowledge laid the foundations for their collection of *Children's and Household Tales*. Other collectors contributed to the two brothers' activities, for instance the poet Annette von Droste-Hülshoff and her sister. Jacob and Wilhelm also took many stories from the French collection of Charles Perrault (1628–1703). "Briar Rose" and "Little Red Cap," for instance, are of French origin.

Jacob and Wilhelm also wrote tales themselves. They extended their collection in later editions, and revised the texts extensively several times, often because readers had objected that the fairy tales were too cruel, and might encourage brutality. The Grimm brothers collected legends as well as fairy tales. The volume containing the *German Legends of the Brothers Grimm* lists 585 titles. One example, "The Children of Hamelin," also known as "The Pied Piper of Hamelin," is included in this book.

The illustrator Lisbeth Zwerger, who has won the highest international distinctions, devoted herself very early to the fairy tale genre, and attracted attention with her surprisingly new vision of the old material. The course of her wide-ranging artistic development can be traced through her work on the tales of the brothers Grimm that are included in this book.

Werner Thusnelder

THE FROG KING
OR IRON HENRY

Once upon a time, when wishes could still come true, there was a king whose daughters were all beautiful, but the youngest was so lovely that the sun itself, although it had seen so much, marvelled at her beauty whenever it shone on her face. Close to the king's castle there was a great, dark forest, and in the forest, under an old linden tree, there was a well. If the weather was very hot, the king's daughter used to go out into the forest and sit on the rim of the well – and if she was bored she took a golden ball that was her favorite plaything with her, threw it up in the air and caught it again.

One day it so happened that after she had thrown the golden ball up it did not fall back into her little hands again, but came down on the ground and rolled straight into the water. The king's daughter followed it with her eyes, but the ball disappeared, and the well was deep, so deep that you couldn't see to the bottom of it. Then she began to weep and wail inconsolably, louder and louder. And as she was weeping like that, a voice spoke to her, "What's the matter, king's daughter? Why are you crying so pitifully that it would melt a heart of stone?"

She looked around to find out where the voice came from, and then she saw a frog putting his fat, ugly head up above the water. "Oh, it's you, is it, old squelchy-splasher?" she said. "I'm crying because my golden ball has fallen into the well, and now I've lost it."

"Hush, don't cry," replied the frog. "I can help you there, but what will you give me if I bring your plaything up out of the water again?"

"Anything you like, dear frog," she said. "My fine dresses, my pearls and jewels, even the golden crown that I wear."

"I don't want your dresses, your pearls and jewels or your golden crown," said the frog, "but if you will be kind to me and take me as your friend and playmate, let me sit at your little table beside you, eat from your little golden plate, drink from your little golden goblet and sleep in your little bed – if you will promise me all that, I will climb down the well and bring your golden ball up again."

"Oh yes," she said, "I promise anything you like if you will only bring me back my golden ball." But she was thinking: what nonsense that silly frog talks! There he sits in the water with the other frogs, so how can he be friends with any human being?

Once she had promised, the frog dipped his head down under the water, sank to the bottom of the well, and a little later he came swimming up again with the ball in his mouth and dropped it on the grass. The king's daughter was delighted to see her pretty toy again. She picked it up and ran away with it.

"Wait for me!" the frog called after her. "Take me with you. I can't run as fast as you!"

But however loud he croaked, it did him no good! She paid him no attention, but hurried home and soon forgot all about the poor frog, who had to climb down into his well again.

Next day, when she was sitting at the dinner table with the king and all the courtiers, eating from her little golden plate, something came crawling up the marble steps outside the castle, slip slop, slip slop, and when it was at the top of the flight of steps it knocked on the door and called, "Youngest daughter of the king, open the door to let me in!" She went to see who was outside the door, but when she opened it, there sat the frog. Then she quickly slammed the door and sat down again, feeling very frightened. The king could see that her heart was beating fast, and he asked, "What are you afraid of, my child? Is there a giant outside the door wanting to take you away?"

"No," she said, "it's not a giant, it's a nasty frog."

"What does the frog want?"

"Oh, dear father, when I was sitting beside the well in the forest yesterday my golden ball fell into the water. And the frog fetched it out because I was crying so hard, and when he insisted I promised to be his friend, but I never thought he could get out of the water. Now he's outside the door and wants to come in."

And already there was a second knock on the door, and a voice called out:

"Youngest king's daughter

Open the door.

Don't you remember

The promise you swore,

Beside the cool water

Youngest king's daughter?

Open the door!"

Then the king said, "If you made a promise, you must keep it, so go and open the door to him." She went and opened the door, and the frog hopped in and followed her back to her chair. He sat there on the floor and said, "Pick me up so that I can sit beside you!" She hesitated until at last the king told her to do as the frog said. Once he was on the chair he wanted to get up on the table, and when he was on the table he said, "Push your little golden plate closer to me so that we can eat from it together."

She did as the frog said, but anyone could tell that she was reluctant to do so. The frog ate a good dinner, but she could hardly swallow a morsel. At last the frog said, "I've eaten all I want, and now I'm tired, so carry me into your little bedchamber, make up the bed with silken sheets, and we'll lie down to sleep."

The king's daughter began to weep, because she was afraid of the cold, clammy frog. She didn't like to touch him, and now she must let him sleep in her lovely, clean little bed. But the king was angry, and said, "If someone helps you in your hour of need, then you must not despise him afterwards." So she picked up the frog with the tips of two fingers, carried him to her bedchamber and put him down in a corner. However, when she was lying in bed he came crawling up and said, "I'm tired, I want to sleep in as much comfort as you, so pick me up or I'll tell your father!"

At that she lost her temper, seized the frog and threw him against the wall with all her might, saying, "That will keep you quiet, you nasty frog!"

However, when he fell to the floor he wasn't a frog any more, he had turned into a king's son with kind and beautiful eyes. And now, as her father the king wished, he was to be her dear friend and her husband. He told her that a wicked witch had cast a spell on him, and no one but the king's youngest daughter could break the spell and release him from the water in the well. Tomorrow, he said, they would go off to his own kingdom together. Then they went to sleep, and at sunrise next morning a carriage drawn by eight white horses came driving up. The horses had white ostrich plumes on their heads, and were harnessed to the carriage with golden chains, and behind the carriage stood the young king's servant, Faithful Henry. Faithful Henry had been so upset when his master was turned into a frog that he had had three iron bands fastened around his heart, to keep it from breaking with misery and sadness. Now that the carriage was to take the young king away to his kingdom, Faithful Henry helped him and his young wife into it, got up behind them again, and was full of joy to see that the spell had been broken.

When they had gone part of the way the king's son heard a cracking noise behind him, like something breaking. So he turned round and called:

"Henry, the carriage is breaking!" But Faithful Henry replied:

"No, sir, that was my heart waking.
Cracking one of the iron bands
Forged around it when from your lands
You were exiled by the witch's spell,
To be a frog and live in a well."

As they drove along there was a second cracking sound, and then a third, and each time the king's son thought the carriage was breaking, but it was only the iron bands falling away from Faithful Henry's heart, because now his master was released from the spell and was happy.

THE WOLF AND THE
SEVEN YOUNG KIDS

Once upon a time there was an old nanny-goat who had seven young kids, and she loved them dearly, just as any mother loves her children. One day, when she wanted to go into the forest and look for food, she called all seven to her and said, "Dear children, I'm going into the forest, so you must be on your guard against the wolf. If he gets into this house he'll eat you all up. He often pretends to be someone else, but you'll know him by his rough voice and his black paws."

"Dear Mother," said the kids, "we'll take good care, so you go out and don't worry about us." So the old goat bleated goodbye and set off with her mind at rest.

It wasn't long before someone knocked at the door of the house and called, "Open the door, dear children, here's your mother back bringing something nice for each of you." But the kids could hear from his rough voice that he was the wolf. "No," they replied, "you're not our mother. She has a kind, gentle voice, but your voice is rough. You're the wolf."

The wolf went away to a shop where he bought a big piece of chalk; he ate it to soften his voice. Then he came back, knocked on the door of the house and called, "Open the door, dear children, here's your mother back bringing something nice for each of you." But the wolf had put one of his black paws on the window-sill, and the goat's children saw it and said, "We won't open the door; our mother doesn't have a black paw like you. You're the wolf."

Then the wolf went to a baker and said, "I've hurt my paw. Put some dough on it, please." And when the baker had spread dough over his paw, he went to the miller and said, "Sprinkle some white flour over my paw." The miller thought: the wolf wants to deceive someone. And he was unwilling to do it, but the wolf said, "If you don't do as I say, I'm going to eat you up." Then the miller was frightened, and made the wolf's paw look white. That's human nature for you.

Now the wicked wolf went to the door of the goat's house for the third time, knocked on the door and said, "Open the door, dear children, here's your mother back bringing something out of the forest for each of you."

"Show us your paw first," called the kids, "so that we'll know if you're really our dear mother."

Then the wolf put his paw on the window-sill, and when they saw that it was white they believed that what he said was true, and opened the door. However, it wasn't

their mother who came in but the wolf. They were frightened, and tried to hide. One of them ran under the table, the second jumped into the bed, the third hid in the stove, the fourth in the kitchen, the fifth in the wardrobe, the sixth under the wash-basin, and the seventh in the case of the clock on the wall. But the wolf found them all and made short work of them: he swallowed them one by one, and the only one he missed was the youngest, who was hiding in the clock case. And when his appetite was satisfied he strolled away, lay down outside in the green grass of the meadow under a tree, and went to sleep.

Not long after that, the old nanny-goat came home from the forest. Oh, what a sight met her eyes! The front door of the house was wide open, the table, chairs and benches were turned upside down, the wash-basin was smashed to pieces, the blanket and pillows had been pulled off the bed. She looked for her children, but they were nowhere to be found. She called their names, one after another, but no one answered. At last, when she came to the name of the youngest, a little voice called, "Dear Mother, I'm here in the clock case on the wall." She let the kid out, and he told her how the wolf had come and eaten all the others. You can imagine how the goat wept for her poor children. At last, in her grief, she went out of the house, and the youngest little kid went with her. When she came to the meadow, there was the wolf lying under the tree, snoring so hard that the branches shook.

She looked at the wolf from all sides, and saw that there was something moving and wriggling inside his big, over-stretched belly. Oh God, she thought, can my poor children still be alive after the wolf swallowed them all for his supper? And she sent the seventh kid running back to the house to fetch her a pair of scissors, a needle and some thread. Then she slit open the monster's belly, and as soon as she had made the first cut one of the kids put his head out, and as she went on cutting all six jumped out, one by one. They were all still alive, and hadn't even come to any harm, because in his greed the monster had swallowed them whole. How happy they were! They hugged their dear mother, and capered about like a tailor on his wedding day.

"Now," said the old nanny-goat, "go and fetch me some big lumps of rock, and we'll fill the wicked creature's belly with those while he's still asleep." So the seven little kids hurried off to find the stones, and put as many inside the wolf's belly as it would take. Then the old nanny-goat quickly sewed it up again, so that the wolf wouldn't notice

anything. He didn't even move while all this was going on.

When the wolf had finally slept long enough, he got up, and because the stones inside him made him feel thirsty he wanted to find a well and drink water from it. However, when he was on his feet and began walking, the stones inside him hit each other as he moved and rumbled around. Then the wolf cried:

"What's rumbling inside me?
What jiggles and thumps?
It ought to be kids,
But it sounds like stone lumps."

And when he came to the well and leaned over the rim of it to drink the water, the heavy stones dragged him in, and he drowned miserably. Seeing his fate, the seven little kids came running up, shouting, "The wolf is dead, the wolf is dead!" Then they and their mother danced around the well for joy.

HANSEL
AND
GRETEL

There was once a poor woodcutter who lived near a large forest with his wife and his two children; the little boy was called Hansel and the little girl's name was Gretel. He did not have much at home for his family to eat, and a time came when prices were so high in the country round about that he couldn't even provide their daily bread. As he lay in bed one evening, tossing and turning as he thought of all his anxieties, he sighed and said to his wife, "What's to become of us? How can we feed our poor children, when we have nothing left to eat ourselves?"

"I'll tell you what to do, husband," his wife replied. "Early tomorrow morning we'll take the children out into the thickest part of the forest; we'll light a fire for them there and give them a piece of bread each, and then we'll go about our work and leave them alone. They'll never find the way home again, and we'll be rid of them."

"No, wife," said her husband. "I won't do that. How could I find it in my heart to take my children into the forest and leave them alone there, where the wild beasts would soon come and tear them to pieces?"

"You fool," she said. "Then all four of us must die of starvation, and all you have to do is plane the planks for our coffins smooth." And she went on pestering him until he agreed. "But I feel so sorry for the poor children," he said.

The two children hadn't been able to sleep either because they were so hungry, and they had heard what their stepmother said to their father. Gretel shed bitter tears and said to Hansel, "It's all up with us now."

"Hush, Gretel," said Hansel. "Don't worry, I'll think of a way to help us." And when the old people had gone to sleep, he got up, put on his little coat, opened the bottom half of the door and stole out. The moon was shining brightly, and the white pebbles outside the house gleamed like silver coins. Hansel bent down and put as many of them in his coat pocket as it would take. Then he went back indoors, and told Gretel, "Cheer up, dear little sister, and go to sleep. God will not abandon us." And he got back into bed.

At daybreak, even before the sun had risen, the woman came to wake the two children. "Get up, you lazybones," she said. "We're going into the forest to fetch wood." Then she gave them each a piece of bread, saying, "That's for you to eat in the middle of the day, but don't eat it any earlier, because it's all you'll get." Gretel put the bread under her apron, because Hansel's pocket was full of pebbles. Then they all set off for the forest together. When they had been walking for a little while, Hansel stopped and

looked back at the house. He did that again and again.

"What are you looking at, Hansel?" asked his father. "Don't lag behind like that, stir your stumps!"

"Oh, Father," said Hansel, "I'm looking at my little white cat sitting on the roof saying goodbye to me."

"Nonsense," said the woman, "that's not your cat, it's the morning sun shining on the chimney." But Hansel had not really been looking at his cat; whenever he had stopped it was to take one of the shiny pebbles out of his pocket and drop it on the path.

When they were in the middle of the forest, the father said, "Off you go to gather wood, children, and I'll light a fire to keep you warm." Hansel and Gretel busily collected a whole pile of twigs, their father lit the fire, and when the flames were burning high the woman said, "Lie down by the fire, children, and have a rest. We're going on into the forest to chop wood. When we've finished our work we'll come back for you."

Hansel and Gretel sat by the fire, and when it was mid-day they ate their bread. And because they could hear the blows of the axe, they thought their father was nearby. However, it was not his axe they heard, but a branch that he had tied to a dry tree, swinging back and forth in the wind. When they had sat like that for a long time, they were so weary that their eyes closed, and they fell fast asleep. At last, much later, they woke up to find that it was dark, and night had fallen.

Gretel began to cry, and said, "How are we going to get out of the forest now?" But Hansel comforted her. "Wait a little while," he said, "until the moon has risen, and then we'll easily find our way." And when the full moon had risen into the sky, Hansel took his little sister's hand and followed the trail of pebbles, which shone like newly minted coins and showed them the way.

They walked all night, and as day was dawning they reached their father's house again. They knocked on the door, and when the woman opened it and saw Hansel and Gretel, she said, "Oh, you naughty children, why did you sleep for so long in the forest? We thought you were never going to come home again." But their father was glad to see them, because it had cut him to the heart to leave them alone like that.

Not long after that, there were great shortages all over the country again, and the children heard their stepmother talking to their father in bed. "We've eaten everything in the house," she said, "and there's only half a loaf of bread left. The children must go.

We'll take them further into the forest this time, so that they'll never find their way out again, or there's no saving ourselves." Her husband was heavy-hearted, and he thought: it would be better for me to share my last crust with my children. But his wife wouldn't listen to him; she scolded him and called him a fool. A man who has said A must say B too, and as he had given way the first time he had to give way again now.

But the children, lying awake, had overheard their conversation. When the old people were asleep Hansel got up again, and he was going out to collect pebbles as he had done before, but the woman had locked the door, and he couldn't get out. However, he comforted his little sister, saying, "Don't cry, Gretel, go to sleep, and the Lord God will help us."

Early in the morning the woman came and got the children out of bed. They were given a piece of bread each, but a smaller piece than last time. On the way to the forest Hansel crumbled his bread in his pocket, and he often stood still and dropped a crumb on the ground.

"Why do you keep stopping to look back, Hansel?" asked his father. "Come along, hurry up."

"I'm looking at my little pigeon sitting on the roof and saying goodbye to me," replied Hansel.

"Nonsense," said the woman. "That's not your pigeon, it's the morning sun shining on the chimney." But Hansel dropped all his crumbs on the path little by little.

The woman took the children even further into the forest this time, to a place where they had never in their lives been before. Once again a big fire was lit for them, and the stepmother said, "Sit there, children, and if you're tired you could sleep for a while. We're going on into the forest to chop wood, and in the evening, when we've done our work, we'll come and fetch you." At mid-day Gretel shared her bread with Hansel, who had crumbled his piece of bread as they walked along. Then they went to sleep, and the evening passed by, but no one came back for the poor children. They didn't wake until it was dark, and night had fallen.

Hansel comforted his little sister, saying, "Just wait until the moon rises, Gretel, and then we'll see the breadcrumbs I dropped showing us the way home." And when the moon rose they set off, but they couldn't find any of the breadcrumbs, because the thousands of birds flying around the forest and the fields had pecked them all up.

"I'm sure we can still find the way," Hansel told Gretel, but they didn't find it. They walked all night, and all the next day from morning to evening, but they couldn't get out of the forest, and they were very hungry, because they had nothing to eat but a few berries growing on the ground. And when they were so tired that their legs would carry them no further, they lay down under a tree and went to sleep.

When they woke up it was the third morning since they had left their father's house. They began walking again, but they only went further and further into the forest, and if they did not find help soon they would surely pine away and die. At mid-day they saw a beautiful snow-white bird sitting on a branch, singing such a lovely song that they stopped to listen. When it had finished its song, it spread its wings and flew ahead of them, and they followed until they came to a little house. The bird settled on its roof, and as they came closer they saw that the house was built of bread and its roof was cake, while the windows were made of clear barley sugar.

"Let's eat something," said Hansel. "We'll have a delicious meal. I'm going to eat a piece of the roof, Gretel, and you can eat a window pane. It will taste so sweet." And he reached up to break a little of the roof off and find out what it tasted like, while Gretel began nibbling a window pane. Then a high voice called out from the parlor inside the house:

"Nibble, nibble, mousie.
Who's nibbling at my housie?"

And the children replied:
"Only the wind so wild,
The wild wind, Heaven's own child,"

and they went on eating; there was no stopping them. Hansel, finding that the roof tasted very good indeed, tore off a large piece of it, and Gretel took out a whole round window pane, sat down and feasted on it.

Then the door suddenly opened, and an old, old woman leaning on a stick came out. Hansel and Gretel were so scared that they dropped what they were holding. But the old woman wagged her head and said, "Why, dear children, who brought you here? Come in, come in and stay with me, and no harm will come to you." She took them both by the hand and led them into her little house. A good meal was set on the table for them, milk and pancakes with sugar, apples and nuts. Then two pretty little beds were made up with white sheets, and Hansel and Gretel lay down in them and thought they were in heaven.

But the old woman, who had only been pretending to be so friendly, was really a wicked witch who lay in wait for children, and she built her little house of bread just to entice children to her. When she had one of them in her power, she would kill, cook and eat the child, and that was a feast day to her. Witches have red eyes and do not see very well, but they have a keen sense of smell, like animals, and they notice when human beings are coming their way. Once Hansel and Gretel were close to her, she cackled with laughter and said scornfully, "I have them now, and they won't get away from me."

Early in the morning, before the children were awake, the witch got up, and seeing their plump, pink cheeks as they slept so sweetly, she murmured, "These two will make good eating." Then she seized Hansel with her skinny hand and carried him out to a little shed with a barred door over it. He could scream as much as he liked in there, but it would do him no good.

Then she went in to Gretel, shook her awake, and said, "Get up, lazybones, fetch water and cook something nice for your brother. He's in the shed outside, and I want to fatten him up. And when he's nice and fat I'm going to eat him." Gretel began shedding bitter tears, but all in vain. She had to do as the wicked witch told her.

So the best of food was cooked for poor Hansel, while Gretel got nothing to eat but the shells of river crayfish. The old woman went to the little shed every morning and said, "Hansel, put your finger through the bars so that I can feel it and see whether you'll soon be fat enough." But Hansel put a bone out through the bars, and because of her bad eyesight the witch couldn't see it. Thinking it was Hansel's finger, she was surprised that he never grew any fatter at all.

At the end of four weeks, when Hansel still felt thin, she lost patience and decided not to wait any longer. "Here, Gretel," she called, "hurry up and fetch water. Whether Hansel is fat or thin, tomorrow I'm going to kill and eat him."

How Hansel's poor little sister wept and wailed when she had to carry the water, and how the tears flowed down her cheeks! "Dear God, help us!" she prayed. "If only the wild beasts in the forest had eaten us, at least we would have died together."

"Never mind your snivelling," said the old woman. "That's not going to help you."

Early next morning Gretel had to go out, hang up a cauldron full of water and light a fire under it. "But first we'll bake," said the old woman. "I've already heated the baking oven and kneaded the dough." She made poor Gretel go out to the baking oven, which already had flames shooting out of it. "Crawl into the oven," said the witch, "and see if it's hot enough yet." But once Gretel was inside the oven she was planning to slam its door, so that Gretel would roast inside it, and then she would eat her as well.

However, Gretel saw what she had in mind, and she said, "I don't know how to do that. How do I get inside the oven?"

"Silly goose," said the old woman, "the opening is big enough. Look, I could crawl into it myself." She went up to the oven and put her head inside it. Then Gretel gave her a push that sent her far into the oven, closed the iron door and bolted it. Oh, how horribly the witch began to howl! But Gretel ran away, and the godless witch burned miserably to death.

As for Gretel, she went straight to Hansel, opened his shed and cried, "Hansel, we're safe, the old witch is dead." Then Hansel leaped out like a bird released from a cage when its door is opened. How happy they were, dancing around and hugging and kissing one another! Now that they had nothing to fear, they went into the witch's house, where there were chests full of pearls and jewels in every corner.

"These are better than pebbles," said Hansel, and he stuffed his pockets with as many as they would hold.

"I'll take some home as well," said Gretel, filling her apron with precious stones.

"But now let's go," said Hansel, "and we'll get out of the witch's forest as soon as we can."

However, when they had walked for a few hours, they came to a great stretch of water. "We can't get across," said Hansel. "I don't see any bridge or causeway."

"And there's no boat here either," said Gretel, "but I see a white duck. If I ask her maybe she will carry us over." And she called:

"Little white duck,

Please bring us luck.

Here we stand, children two.

Take us across the water with you."

Then the duck swam over, and Hansel sat on her back and told his sister to join him.

"No," said Gretel, "we'll be too heavy for the duck, both of us together. I'm sure she will take us over one after the other."

And so the good little creature did, and when they were safely over the water, and had walked a little way, the forest looked to them more and more familiar, and at last they saw their father's house in the distance. Then they began to run, raced into the parlor and flung their arms around their father. He had not had a moment's happiness since leaving his children in the forest. As for his wife, she had died. Gretel tipped out the contents of her apron, so that the pearls and jewels rolled over the parlor floor, and Hansel added handful after handful from his pocket. Then all their troubles were over, and they lived happily together.

That's the end of my story – and there runs a mouse! Anyone who catches it can make a big fur cap of it.

THE BRAVE
LITTLE TAILOR

One summer morning a little tailor was sitting on his table at the window, in great good spirits, stitching away for all he was worth. Then a peasant woman came down the street, calling, "Good jam for sale! Good jam for sale!"

That sounded nice to the tailor, and he put his little head out of the window and called, "Come up here, good woman, and you'll find a market for your wares."

The woman carried her heavy basket up the three flights of stairs to the tailor's workshop, and she had to unpack all the jars in front of him. He examined them, held them up to the light, sniffed them, and at last he said, "This looks like good jam. Weigh me out four ounces, my good woman, and I don't mind if you make it quarter of a pound."

The woman, who had hoped to sell a great deal more, gave him what he wanted, but she went away in a bad temper, grumbling.

"Well, God bless this jam," cried the little tailor, "and give me strength and power." He took bread out of his cupboard, cut himself a slice right across the loaf, and spread it with the jam. "That will taste sweet," said he, "but I'll finish making this doublet before I taste it."

He put the slice of bread down beside him and went on sewing, taking bigger and bigger stitches in his delight. Meanwhile, the smell of the sweet jam rose up the wall, where a great many flies had settled, enticing them to come down and settle on it in swarms. "Hey, who invited you?" said the tailor, shooing his unwanted guests away. However, the flies, who didn't speak his language, were not to be deterred, and they came back, more and more of them. In the end the tailor lost his temper, went to his broom cupboard and found a cloth. "You just wait, I'll show you!" said he, bringing it mercilessly down on the flies. When he took it away and counted the flies on it, no fewer than seven lay there dead before him with their legs in the air.

Well, what a fine fellow you are! he told himself, admiring his own courage. The whole town shall hear of this! And in haste the tailor cut out a belt for himself, sewed it together, and embroidered the words "Seven At A Blow" on it in large letters. The town, did I say? he went on. No, the whole world shall hear of it! And his heart hopped for joy like a lamb wagging its tail. The tailor put the belt around his waist and prepared to set out into the world, because he thought his workshop too small for a man so bold. Before he left, he searched the house to see if there was anything he could take with him,

but all he found was an old cheese, which he put in his pocket. Outside the gate he noticed a bird caught in a bush, and the bird went into his pocket with the cheese.

Now he strode bravely along the road, and as he was light on his feet and agile he did not feel tired. The road led to a mountain, and when he had reached the highest peak of it he found a mighty giant sitting there, looking around at his ease. The little tailor went cheerfully up to him and spoke to him, saying, "Good day, comrade. Am I right in thinking that you're sitting there looking at the whole wide world? I'm on the way there myself to try my luck. Would you like to go along with me?"

The giant looked scornfully at the tailor and said, "You scoundrel! You miserable little fellow!"

"What a thing to say!" replied the tailor, unbuttoning his coat and showing the giant his belt. "Read that, and you'll see what kind of a man I am."

The giant read "Seven At A Blow", and thinking it meant that the tailor had killed seven men with a single blow he felt some respect for the little fellow. But he wanted to test him first. So he picked up a stone and squeezed it in his hand until water dripped out.

"You do that too," said the giant, "if you're really so strong."

"Is that all?" said the tailor. "It's child's play to the likes of me." With these words he put his hand into his pocket, took out the soft cheese, and pressed it until the whey ran out. "That was rather better, don't you agree?"

The giant didn't know what to say, and he didn't really believe in the little man. So he took a stone and threw it so high in the air that it almost disappeared from view.

"Now then, you dwarf, do that too."

"Well thrown," said the tailor, "but the stone will have fallen to earth again somewhere. I'll throw one so high that it never comes back at all." So saying, he put his hand in his pocket, took out the bird and threw it up in the air. Glad to be free, the bird rose in the air, flew away and didn't come back. "How do you like that trick, comrade?" asked the tailor.

"You can throw well," said the giant, "but now let's see if you can carry a good weight." And he led the little tailor to a mighty oak tree that had been felled and was lying on the ground. "If you're strong enough," he said, "help me to carry this tree out of the wood."

"Happily," said the little man. "You just take the trunk on your shoulder, and I'll pick up the branches with all their twigs and carry them. They're the heaviest part."

So the giant took the trunk on his shoulder, but the tailor sat on a branch, and the giant, who couldn't see behind him, had to carry the whole tree and the tailor into the bargain. As for the tailor, he sat there behind his companion in great good spirits, whistling the tune of "Three Tailors Went Riding Away From The Gate", as if carrying a tree were child's play. After the giant had carried the heavy weight of the tree some way further, he could not go on, and called, "Listen, I'll have to drop this tree." The tailor nimbly jumped down, flung his arms round the tree as if he had been carrying it, and said to the giant, "What, a great big fellow like you, and you can't even carry a tree?"

They went on together, and as they were passing a cherry tree the giant took hold of the crown, where the earliest ripe fruits hung, bent it down, put it in the tailor's hand and told him to enjoy the cherries. However, the tailor was far too weak to hold the tree down, and when the giant let go the tree-top shot up in the air again, taking the tailor with it. When he had dropped back to the ground without suffering any injury, the giant said, "What is it? Aren't you strong enough to hold that weak little shoot down?"

"Oh, I'm not short of strength," said the little tailor. "Do you think that would be any problem for a man who has killed seven at a blow? No, I jumped over the tree because there are huntsmen firing guns in the bushes down there. You jump over it yourself if you can."

The giant tried, but he couldn't leap over the tree, and stuck fast in the branches, so once again the little tailor got the better of him.

Then the giant said, "If you're such a bold fellow, come and spend the night in our cavern with us."

The little tailor agreed to that, and followed him. When they reached the cavern some more giants were sitting by the fire, each eating a whole roast sheep that he held in his hands. The tailor looked around and thought: this is a much more spacious place than my workshop at home.

The giant showed him a bed and told him to lie down in it and have a good sleep. But the bed was too big for the little tailor, and he didn't lie down there but crept into a corner. At midnight, when the giant thought the little tailor must be fast asleep, he got up, took a big iron bar, struck the bed in half with a single blow, and thought he had put an end to that annoying little grasshopper the tailor.

Early in the morning the giants went into the woods, forgetting all about the tailor, when all of a sudden he came strolling boldly and cheerfully along. The startled giants were afraid he would strike them all dead, and they ran away as fast as they could go.

The little tailor went on, always following his pointed nose. When he had walked for a long time, he came to a royal palace, and as he felt tired he lay down on the grass in the courtyard and fell asleep. While he was lying there some courtiers came along, looked at him from all sides, and read what it said on his belt. "Seven At A Blow."

"What can this heroic warrior be doing here in peace-time?" they said. "He must be a mighty lord."

They went and told the king, saying that if war happened to break out, this would be an important and useful man, and they ought to keep him with them at all costs. The king liked this advice, and he sent one of the courtiers off to see the little tailor when he woke up, and offer him service in any wars.

The king's envoy stood beside the sleeping tailor, waited until he stretched and opened his eyes, and then made his offer.

"That's the very reason why I came here," replied the little tailor. "I'm ready and willing to enter the service of the king." So he was welcomed with honor, and given special apartments of his own.

However, the king's soldiers didn't like the idea of the little tailor, and wished him a thousand miles away.

"What's going to happen," they said to each other, "if we argue with him and he fights us? Seven of us will fall at every blow! We can't stand up to losses like that."

So they came to a decision, went to the king together, and asked to be dismissed from the army. "We can't compete with a man who kills seven at a blow," they said.

The king was very sorry to think of losing all his faithful servants for the sake of a single man. He wished he had never set eyes on the hero, and would have liked to be rid of him again. But he didn't trust himself to dismiss the great warrior, being afraid the tailor might kill him and all his people and seize the throne for himself. He thought long and hard, and at last he had an idea. He sent a message to the tailor to say that as he was such a heroic warrior, he, the king, would make him an offer. There were two giants at large in a forest in his country, doing great damage, robbing, murdering,

burning and laying the countryside waste. No one could get near them without putting himself in deadly danger. If he could overcome and kill those two giants, said the king, he would give him his only daughter as his wife, and half the kingdom as her dowry. He could also have a hundred horsemen to go with him and give him their aid.

That would be a fine thing for a man like me, thought the little tailor. You don't get offered a king's beautiful daughter and half his kingdom every day of the week.

"Why, certainly," he replied. "I'll deal with the giants, and I don't really need the hundred horsemen. A man who can kill seven at a blow will hardly be afraid of two."

So the little tailor set out, and the hundred horsemen followed him. When he came to the outskirts of the forest, he said to his companions, "You can stay here and leave the giants to me."

Then he leaped into the forest, looking to right and left as he went. After a while he saw the two giants. They were lying asleep under a tree, snoring so hard that the branches swayed up and down. The little tailor, wasting no time, filled both his pockets with stones and climbed the tree. When he was in the middle of the crown, he slid along a branch until he was sitting just above the sleeping giants, and he dropped stones, one after another, on the first giant's chest. For some time the giant felt nothing, but at last he woke up, nudged his companion and said, "Hey, why are you hitting me?"

"You're dreaming," said the other giant. "I never hit you."

They lay down to go back to sleep, and then the tailor threw a stone down on the second giant.

"What's the idea?" asked the second giant. "Why are you throwing stones at me?"

"I'm not throwing anything at you," growled the first giant in reply.

They argued for a while, but since they were tired they let the subject drop, and their eyes closed again. The little tailor began his game again from the beginning. He chose his biggest stone and threw it as hard as he could at the first giant's chest.

"Oh, this is too bad!" cried the giant, jumping up like a madman, and he pushed his companion up against the tree so hard that its trunk shook. The second giant repaid him in the same coin, and they fell into such a rage that they tore up tree after tree and hit out at each other until at last they both fell down dead.

Now the little tailor jumped down.

"What luck," he said, "that they didn't uproot the tree where I was sitting, or I'd

have had to jump to another like a squirrel. But a man like me is quick on his feet."
He drew his sword and drove it hard a couple of times into both the giants' chests,
and then he went back to the horsemen and said, "The job's done. I've put an end to
both those giants, but it was a hard fight. In their desperation they tore up trees to defend
themselves, but that's no use against a man like me who can kill seven at a blow."

"Aren't you wounded at all?" asked the horsemen.

"Not a bit of it," replied the tailor. "They never hurt a hair of my head."

The horsemen couldn't believe him, and rode into the wood, where they found the
giants lying in their own blood, with uprooted trees lying around them.

Now the tailor asked the king for the promised reward. The king, however, regretted
his promise, and once again he wondered how he could rid himself of the hero.

"Before you get my daughter and half the kingdom," he said, "you must do one
more heroic deed. There's a unicorn running wild in the forest, doing a great deal of
damage. First you must catch the unicorn."

"I'm even less afraid of a unicorn than of two giants. Seven at a blow is all in the
day's work for me." So saying, he took a rope and an axe with him, went out into the
forest, and told the men who were escorting him to stay behind. He didn't have to
search for long before the unicorn appeared, racing straight towards the tailor as if to
impale him on its horn.

"Take it easy," he said. "You're going about this too fast." He stood there and waited
until the animal was very close, and then dodged nimbly behind the tree. The unicorn
ran at the tree with all its might, burying its horn so firmly in the tree trunk that it
didn't have the strength to pull it out again, and so the tailor caught it. "I have you
now, birdie," he said, coming out from behind the tree. First he put his rope around the
unicorn's neck, then he hacked the horn out of the tree with his axe, and when all that
was done he led the animal away and took it to the king.

But the king still didn't want to give him the promised reward, and he made a
third condition. Before the wedding, he said, the tailor must catch a wild boar that was
ravaging the forest, doing a great deal of damage. The court huntsmen, he told the tailor,
would be with him to lend him their aid.

"Willingly," said the tailor. "That's child's play."

He didn't take the huntsmen into the forest with him, and they were heartily glad of that, because the wild boar had faced them so fiercely several times before that they did not in the least want to hunt the creature.

When the boar saw the tailor, it ran at him, foaming at the mouth and whetting its tusks, intending to throw him to the ground. However, our nimble hero leaped into a nearby chapel and straight out of the window again with a single bound. The wild boar had run into the chapel after him, but the tailor hurried round outside and slammed the door. The furious animal, being much too heavy and clumsy to jump out of the window itself, was trapped. Now the tailor called to the huntsmen to come and see the captive boar with their own eyes. Meanwhile the hero himself went to the king who now, like it or not, had to keep his promise and give the tailor his daughter and half the kingdom. If he had known that a little tailor and not a heroic warrior stood there before him, he would have regretted it even more. So the wedding was celebrated with great magnificence but little joy, and the tailor became a king.

After some time the young queen heard her husband talking in his sleep by night, when he was dreaming. "Boy," said he, "finish that doublet and mend my trousers or I'll break my yardstick over your head." That told her where the young gentleman came from, and next morning she complained to her father, asking him to rid her of a husband who was nothing but a tailor. The king comforted her, and said, "Leave your bedroom door unlocked tonight. My servants will be posted outside, and when your husband is asleep they will go in, bind him hand and foot, and put him on board a ship that will take him out into the wide world."

The tailor's wife was satisfied with that, but the king's armor-bearer, who liked his young master, had overheard it all and told him about the plot.

"I'll soon put a stop to that," said the little tailor, and that evening he lay down in bed with his wife at the usual time. When she thought he had gone to sleep, she got up, unlocked the door and lay down again. The little tailor, who was only pretending to be asleep, began calling out in a loud voice, "Boy, finish that doublet and mend my trousers or I'll break my yardstick over your head. I've struck down seven at a blow, I've killed two giants, led a unicorn out of the forest and caught a wild boar, and am I going to be afraid of the men standing outside this bedroom?"

When the king's servants heard the tailor talk like that, they were terrified and ran as if the wild hunt were after them. And no one ever dared try to harm him again.

So now the tailor was a king, and a king he remained for the rest of his days.

THE SEVEN RAVENS

There was once a man who had seven sons but no daughter yet, however dearly he wished for one. At last his wife gave him good reason to hope for another child, and when the baby was born it was a girl. The couple were overjoyed, but the child was small and sickly, and had to be given immediate baptism because she was so weak. Her father sent one of the boys in haste, to fetch water from the well for her baptism; the other six brothers went with him, and because each of them wanted to be the first to draw water they were jostling each other, and the jug they had brought fell into the well.

So there they stood, and didn't know what to do. None of them dared to go home. When they didn't come back their father was impatient, and said, "I'm sure those godless boys have been playing some game and forgotten about the water." He was afraid that the little girl would die unbaptised, and he cried in anger, "I wish those boys were all turned into ravens!" As soon as he had spoken those words, he heard a whirring in the air above his head, looked up, and saw seven pitch-black ravens rise from the ground and fly away.

The parents couldn't undo the wish now, and sad as they were to lose their seven sons they found some comfort in their dear little daughter, who quickly recovered her health and grew up to be more beautiful every day. For a long time she didn't even know that she had ever had brothers, because her mother and father were careful not to mention them, until one day, by chance, she overheard people talking about her, saying that she was certainly a beautiful girl, but her seven brothers' misfortune was really her fault. Then she was very sad, went to her father and mother and asked if she had ever had brothers, and what had become of them. Now her parents couldn't keep the secret any longer, but they told her it was Heaven's will, and her birth had been only the innocent cause of it. However, the story weighed on the girl's mind every day, and she decided that she must break the spell on her brothers. She could not rest until she set off in secret to go out into the wide world, track down her brothers wherever they might be, and break the spell on them at any price. She took nothing with her but a little ring as a memento of her parents, a loaf of bread to satisfy her hunger, a jug of water to quench her thirst, and a little chair to sit on when she felt tired.

The girl went on and on, a long, long way, all the way to the end of the world. Then she came to the Sun, but the Sun was hot and fierce and ate children. The girl

hurried away and went to the Moon, but the Moon was cold and cruel and evil, and said, on seeing the child, "I smell human flesh." Then she went away in a hurry, and came to the Stars, who were kind to her. They were all of them sitting on their own little chairs, but the Morning Star stood up, gave the girl a chicken bone and said, "Your brothers are in the glass mountain, and you will need this chicken bone to unlock it."

The girl took the little bone, wrapped it up well in a piece of cloth, and went on her way until she came to the glass mountain. The gate was locked, and she was going to take out the chicken bone, but when she undid the piece of cloth it was empty. She had lost her present from the kindly Stars. What was she to do now? She wanted to save her brothers, but she had no chicken bone to let her into the glass mountain. So the good little sister took a knife, cut off one of her little fingers, put it in the keyhole, and the gate opened easily.

When she had gone through the gateway, a little dwarf came to meet her, saying, "What are you looking for, my child?"

"I'm looking for my brothers the seven ravens," she replied.

"My masters the ravens are not at home," said the dwarf, "but if you would like to wait for them, come in."

Then the dwarf brought in the meal he had prepared for the ravens, served it out on seven little plates, poured their drink into seven little goblets, and their sister ate a morsel from every plate and drank a sip from every goblet, but she dropped the ring she had brought from home into the last little goblet.

Suddenly she heard a whirring and a rushing in the air, and the dwarf said, "Here come my masters the ravens flying home." They came in, went to the table to eat and drink, and looked at their little plates and their little goblets. And they said, one after another, "Who's been eating from my plate? Who's been drinking from my goblet? Some human mouth has been here!"

But when the seventh came to the bottom of his goblet, the ring rolled towards him, and he recognized it as a ring that had belonged to his father and mother. "If only our little sister were here, then God willing, the spell on us would be broken."

The girl was hiding behind the door and listening. On hearing that, she came forward, and all the ravens returned to human form. They and their sister hugged and kissed one another, and they went happily home.

LITTLE RED CAP

Once upon a time there was a dear little girl, and everyone who set eyes on her loved her, but her grandmother loved her most of all, and never tired of giving her presents. Once she gave her granddaughter a little red velvet cap, and because it suited the girl so well, and she wore it all the time, she was known as Little Red Cap.

One day her mother said to her, "Now, Little Red Cap, here's a piece of cake and a bottle of wine. Take them to your grandmother. She's sick and weak and the cake and wine will do her good. You had better set out before the day is too hot, and when you are away from here follow the path like a good girl, or you might fall and break the glass bottle, and there would be none of the wine left for your grandmother. And when you reach her house, don't forget to say good morning, and don't go poking about in every corner!"

"I'll do everything just as you say," Little Red Cap told her mother, giving her hand to show she meant it. Her grandmother, however, lived out in the forest, half an hour's walk from the village, and when Little Red Cap entered the forest the wolf came to meet her. However, she didn't know what a wicked animal he was, so she was not afraid of him.

"Good day, Little Red Cap!" said the wolf.

"Thank you, wolf, and good day to you!" she replied.

"Where are you going so early in the morning, Little Red Cap?"

"To see my grandmother."

"And what's that you are carrying under your apron?"

"Cake and wine. It was baking day yesterday, and I'm taking my poor sick grandmother something to do her good and give her new strength."

"So where does your grandmother live, Little Red Cap?"

"Another quarter of an hour's walk into the forest from here. Her house stands under the three big oak trees with hazel-nut hedges outside it, I'm sure you know the place," said Little Red Cap.

The wolf thought to himself: this tender young thing will make me a good meal; she'll taste even better than the old lady. I must go about this cunningly if I'm to snap them both up. So he went along beside the little girl for a while, and then he said, "Look at those pretty flowers growing all around, Little Red Cap. Why don't you look over there? I don't think you even hear the little birds singing so sweetly. You just walk straight ahead as if you were on your way to school, yet it's such fun out in the forest."

Little Red Cap opened her eyes wide, and when she saw the sunbeams dancing back and forth as they shone through the trees, and all the lovely flowers growing in the

forest, she thought: if I take Grandmother a bunch of fresh flowers she'd like that, too. And it's so early in the day that I shall still arrive in good time. So she left the path through the forest and went looking for flowers. Whenever she picked one, she thought she saw an even prettier one further away, and she went to pick it and so strayed further and further into the forest. But as for the wolf, he went straight to Grandmother's house and knocked on the door.

"Who's that outside?" called the old lady.

"It's me, Little Red Cap, bringing you some cake and wine. Open the door!"

"Just push the latch down," Grandmother replied. "I'm too weak to get up."

The wolf pushed the latch down, the door opened, and without a word he went straight to Grandmother's bed and swallowed her all up. Then he put on her clothes, set her cap on his head, lay down in her bed and drew the curtains round it.

Meanwhile Little Red Cap had been running about picking flowers, and when she had so many that she could hardly carry them she remembered her grandmother, and set off for her house. She was surprised to find the door open, and when she went into Grandmother's room it felt so strange that she said to herself: oh, my goodness, how frightened I feel today, and yet I usually love going to see Grandmother!

"Good morning," she called, but there was no answer. So she went up to the bed and pulled back the curtains. There lay Grandmother with her cap far down over her face, looking so strange.

"Oh, Grandmother, what big ears you have!" "All the better to hear you with!"

"Oh, Grandmother, what big eyes you have!" "All the better to see you with!"

"Oh, Grandmother, what big hands you have!" "All the better to grab you with!"

"But oh, Grandmother, what a terribly big muzzle you have!"

"All the better to eat you with!" And as soon as the wolf had said those words he jumped out of bed and swallowed poor Little Red Cap all up.

When the wolf had satisfied his appetite, he lay down in bed again, fell asleep and began snoring loudly. The huntsman happened to be passing the house, and he thought: how the old lady is snoring! I'd better go and see if there's anything wrong with her. So he went into the room, and when he was standing beside the bed he saw the wolf in it. "Oho, you old sinner, is this where I find you?" said he. "I've been after you for a long time."

And he was about to aim his gun when it occurred to him that the wolf might have swallowed Grandmother whole, and she could still be saved. So he didn't fire a

shot, but took a pair of scissors and began slitting the sleeping wolf's belly open. After he had made a few cuts he saw the little bright red cap, and after a few more the little girl jumped out, crying, "Oh, how scared I was! It was so dark inside the wolf." Then out came her old grandmother as well, still alive but very breathless. Little Red Cap hurried off to fetch some large stones, and they filled the wolf's body with the stones. When he woke up he tried to run away, but the stones were so heavy that he sank under their weight and fell down dead.

They were all three very happy. The huntsman skinned the wolf and took the wolf skin home with him; Grandmother ate the cake and drank the wine that Little Red Cap had brought and soon felt better; and as for Little Red Cap, she thought to herself: I'll never in my life stray off the path and go into the forest when my mother has told me not to.

And there is another story about Little Red Cap. It says that once, when she was taking some cakes to her old grandmother again, another wolf spoke to her and tried to tempt her to leave the path. But Little Red Cap was careful to do no such thing. She went on her way, and told her grandmother how she had met a wolf who wished her good day, but gave her such a nasty look that, she said, "If it hadn't happened in the middle of the road I'm sure he'd have eaten me up."

"Come along," said Grandmother. "We'll close the door so that he can't get in."

Soon the wolf came along, knocked on the door and called, "Open the door, Grandmother. Here I am, Little Red Cap, bringing you some cakes."

But they kept quiet and didn't open the door. The grey wolf prowled round the house several times, and at last he jumped up on the roof, planning to wait until Little Red Cap went home in the evening. Then he was going to follow her and eat her under cover of darkness.

However, Grandmother guessed what he had in mind. There was a big stone trough outside the house, and she said to the little girl, "Take the bucket, Little Red Cap. I boiled some sausages yesterday, so pour the water they were cooked in out into the trough!" Little Red Cap carried out sausage water until the big, big trough was full. The smell of sausages rose to the wolf's nose. He sniffed, he peered down, and at last he craned his neck so far that he lost his footing and began sliding. So he slid right off the roof, straight into the big trough, and he drowned there. But Little Red Cap went happily home, and after that no one did anything to hurt her.

THE BREMEN
TOWN MUSICIANS

Once upon a time a man owned a donkey who had carried sacks to the mill patiently for many long years. However, the donkey's strength was failing now, and he could do less and less work, so his master was thinking of getting rid of him.

Guessing what was in the air, the donkey ran away and set out for Bremen, where he thought he could join the town band as a musician.

When he had been trotting along for a while he met a dog lying in the road, breathing heavily as if he had been running and was quite worn out. "Why are you panting like that, Grabber?" asked the donkey.

"Oh," said the dog, "it's because I'm old, and getting weaker every day. I'm no use for hunting now, and my master was going to kill me. I ran away, but how am I going to earn my living?"

"I'll tell you what," said the donkey, "I'm off to Bremen to be a town musician. Why don't you come with me and join the band too? I'll play the lute, and you can beat the drums."

The dog thought that sounded like a good idea, so they went along together.

It wasn't long before they saw a cat sitting by the roadside, looking as miserable as three days of rainy weather. "So what's the matter with you, old Whiskers?" asked the donkey.

"When people are after your life it's no laughing matter," said the cat. "I'm growing old, my teeth aren't as sharp as they were, and I'd rather sit by the stove and purr than hunt mice, so my mistress tried to drown me. I ran away, but now I don't know what to do. Where am I to go?"

"Join us and come to Bremen," said the donkey. "You're used to singing serenades, so you can be a town musician when we get there."

The cat liked that idea, and he went along with them. On the road the three runaways passed a farm where a cockerel was sitting on the gate, crowing for all he was worth.

"Your crowing is fit to wake the dead," said the donkey.

"Why is that?"

"I was foretelling good weather," said the cockerel, "but tomorrow is Sunday, and because some guests are coming to dinner the farmer's cruel wife has told the cook to make chicken broth of me. I'm to have my head cut off this evening, and I'm crowing

my heart out while I still can."

"I tell you what, Redcrest," said the donkey, "why not come with us instead? We're on our way to Bremen, and you're bound to find something better than death there. You have a fine voice, and if we all make music together we're sure to get by."

But the town of Bremen was too far off for them to reach it in a day, and when they came to a forest that evening they decided to spend the night there. The donkey and the dog settled down under a large tree, the cat and the cockerel climbed up into the branches, and the cockerel flew to the very top of the tree, the safest place for him. Before going to sleep he looked all around him again, and he thought he saw a tiny spark in the distance. He called down to tell his friends that there must be a house not far off, because he could see a light shining.

"Then let's go and find that house," said the donkey. "It's not very comfortable out here." And the dog thought that if he could find a couple of bones with a little meat left on them it would do him good. So they set off for the place where the cockerel had seen the spark, and soon the light was shining more clearly. It grew brighter and brighter until they came to a robbers' house, all lit up inside. The donkey, who was the largest of them, went up to the house and peered through the window.

"What do you see, Greycoat?" asked the cockerel.

"Oh, my word!" said the donkey. "I see a table laid with delicious things to eat and drink, and robbers sitting there feasting and making merry."

"We could do with some of that feast ourselves," said the cockerel.

"Hee-haw, oh yes, how I wish we were in there!" said the donkey.

Then the animals tried to think of a way to chase the robbers out of the house, and in the end they thought of a plan. The donkey propped his front legs on the windowsill, the dog jumped on the donkey's back, the cat climbed up on the dog, and finally the cockerel flew up in the air and perched on the cat's head. When they were ready, a signal was given and everyone began making music:

The donkey brayed, the dog barked, the cat meowed, and the cockerel crowed. Then they jumped into the room through the window, and the glass broke as it crashed to the floor. The robbers leaped up when they heard that terrible loud noise, thinking it was a ghost coming in, and they ran away into the forest, scared out of their wits.

So the four friends sat down at the table, helped themselves to all that was left of

the feast, and ate as if they might go hungry for the next four weeks.

When the four musicians had finished they put out the light and went to find places to sleep, each looking for somewhere comfortable that suited him. The donkey lay down on the rubbish heap, the dog lay behind the door, the cat settled on the stove among the warm ashes, and the cockerel perched on the top rafter of the roof. As they were very tired after their long journey, they soon fell asleep.

After midnight, when the robbers out in the forest saw that there was no light in the house any more, and all seemed quiet, the robber captain said, "We were fools to run away in such a fright." So he told one of his men to go back and search the house. The man he had sent found nothing stirring, and went into the kitchen for a light. He thought that the cat's fiery eyes, glowing in the dark, were live coals, and he held a match to them to set them burning.

But the cat didn't care for that and leaped at his face, spitting and scratching. Terrified, the robber tried to escape through the back door, but the dog lying there jumped up and bit his leg. As he was crossing the yard and running past the rubbish heap, the donkey gave him a powerful kick with his back leg, and as for the cockerel, roused by all this noise and wide awake, he called down from the rafter, "Cock-a-doo-dle-do!"

The robber ran back to his captain as fast as he could go, shouting, "There's a horrible witch in the house who hissed at me and scratched my face with her long fingernails. And a man with a knife at the door stabbed me in the leg, and a big black monster lying in the yard hit me with a wooden cudgel, and up on the roof sits the judge shouting,

'Bring the villain into court!' So I ran for it and made my getaway."

After that the robbers dared not go back to their house.

As for the four Bremen town musicians, they liked it so much that they never left again.

And the last man to tell this tale isn't dead yet.

BRIAR ROSE

Long ago there lived a king and a queen who said to each other every day, "Oh, if only we had a child!" But still they had no children. Then it so happened that one day, when the queen was bathing, a frog crawled up on land out of the water and told her, "Your wish will be granted. Before a year is up you will bring a daughter into the world."

What the frog had said came true, and the queen had a little girl who was so beautiful that the king could hardly contain his delight, and he arranged a great banquet. He invited not only his relations, friends and acquaintances but also the wise women of the country, so that they would look kindly on the baby. There were thirteen wise women in his kingdom, but he had only twelve gold plates for them to eat from, so one of them would have to stay at home.

The feast was celebrated with great magnificence, and when it was over the wise women presented the child with their wonderful gifts: one gave her virtue, the second beauty, the third wealth, and so on, giving her everything that anyone can hope for in this world. When eleven of them had made their wishes for her, the thirteenth suddenly came in. She wanted to get her revenge for not being invited, and without a civil greeting or even a glance for anyone, she cried in a loud voice: "In her fifteenth year the king's daughter will prick her finger on a spindle and fall down dead." And without another word, she turned and left the hall.

All the guests were shocked. Then the twelfth wise woman, who had not yet made her wish, stepped forward, and since she could not break the wicked spell but only make it milder she said, "The king's daughter will fall down not dead, but into a deep sleep lasting a hundred years."

The king, hoping to preserve his dear child from this misfortune, ordered all spindles in his entire kingdom to be burnt. However, the wise women's gifts to the girl all came true, for she was so beautiful, well-behaved, friendly and intelligent that everyone who saw her loved her.

As it happened, on her fifteenth birthday the king and queen were not at home, and the girl was all alone in the castle. She went all over it, into every room and chambers, and at last she came to an old tower. She climbed the narrow spiral staircase, and reached a small door. There was a rusty key in the lock, and when she turned it the door sprang open and she saw an old woman sitting in a little room with a spindle, busily spinning flax.

"Good day, old mother," said the king's daughter. "What are you doing?"

"I'm spinning," said the old woman, nodding her head,

"And what's that thing jumping about in such a funny way?" asked the girl, and she took the spindle to try spinning for herself. But as soon as she had touched the spindle the magic spell came true, and she pricked her finger. At the moment when she felt it prick her, she dropped on the bed standing in the room and lay there in a deep sleep.

That sleep spread over the whole castle. The king and queen, who had just come home and entered the castle hall, fell asleep, and all the courtiers with them. The horses slept in their stables, the dogs slept in the yard, the pigeons on the roof, the flies on the wall. Even the fire flickering on the hearth burned low and went to sleep. The roast meat turning on the spit stopped sizzling, and the cook, who was about to pull the kitchen boy's hair for something he had done wrong, let go of him and fell asleep. The wind died down, and not a leaf stirred on the trees outside the castle. But a thorn hedge began growing round the castle, taller and taller every year, and at last it had surrounded the building entirely and grown right over it, so that nothing was to be seen, not even the flag on top of the roof.

However, the country people told stories of the beautiful sleeping Briar Rose, for that was the name of the king's daughter, and so from time to time kings' sons came and tried to get through the hedge and reach the castle. None of them could do it, because the thorns held together as if they had hands, and the young men were caught in the tangled hedge, could not free themselves, and died a miserable death.

After many years another king's son came into that country and heard an old man telling the tale of the thorn hedge, saying that there was supposed to be a castle behind it where Briar Rose, the beautiful daughter of a king, had slept for a hundred years, and with her the king and queen and all their court. The old man had also heard, from his grandfather, that many kings' sons had already come trying to make their way through the thorny hedge, but they had been caught there and died a tragic death. Then the young man said, "I'm not afraid. I'll go there and see the lovely Briar Rose." However hard the good old man tried to persuade him to give up such an idea, he wouldn't listen.

Now it so happened that the hundred years were up, and the day had come for Briar Rose to awaken to life again. When the king's son approached the thorny hedge, it was

covered with large and beautiful flowers that parted of their own accord and let him through unharmed, and they closed into a hedge again behind him. He saw the horses and the hounds with their pied coats lying asleep in the yard, and the pigeons sitting on the roof with their heads under their wings. And when he was inside the castle he saw the flies asleep on the wall, the cook in the kitchen still raising his hand as if to seize the boy, and the maid sitting with a black chicken that she had been about to pluck on her lap.

Then he went on, and saw the whole court lying in the great hall asleep, while the king and queen lay beside the throne on its dais. He went on and on, and all was so still that you could hear yourself breathing, and at last he came to the tower and opened the door to the little room where Briar Rose was sleeping. There she lay, so beautiful that he couldn't take his eyes off her, and he bent down and gave her a kiss.

When his kiss had touched her, Briar Rose opened her eyes, woke up, and looked at him very kindly. They went down the spiral staircase together, and the king awoke, and so did the queen and all their court, gazing at one another wide-eyed. The horses in the yard stood up and shook themselves; the hounds raced about wagging their tails; the pigeons on the roof took their heads out from under their wings, looked around and flew out into the fields. The flies on the wall crawled on; the fire in the kitchen flickered, burned higher and cooked the meal; the joint on the spit went on sizzling; the cook gave the boy such a slap that he cried out; and the maid finished plucking the chicken. Then the wedding of the king's son to Briar Rose was celebrated with great splendor, and they lived happily together all their lives.

The Poor Miller's Boy
and the Little Cat

There was once an old miller who had neither wife nor children, but lived in his mill with three miller's boys working for him. When they had worked for him for several years, the miller said to them one day, "I'm an old man and feel like taking my ease behind the stove these days. You three lads go out into the world, and I will give the mill to whichever of you brings me back the best horse. In return I'll expect to be looked after here until I die."

The third of the boys was the youngest and smallest, and the other two thought him a simpleton. They didn't want to let him have any chance of getting the mill. So when the three of them set out together, the two older miller's boys said to simple Hans, "You might as well stay here – you'll never in your life come by a horse!"

But Hans went with them all the same. When night fell they came to a cave and crawled into it to sleep there. The two clever boys waited until Hans had fallen asleep, and then they got up and secretly stole away. They left Hans lying there, and thought they had played a clever trick on him. However, it didn't turn out as they expected at all!

When the sun rose and Hans awoke, he was lying in the deep cave. He looked around him and exclaimed, "Dear God, where am I?" At last he sat up, crawled out of the cave, went into the forest and thought: I'm all alone in the world now, the others have abandoned me – and how will I ever come to get a horse?

As he walked along, deep in thought, he suddenly saw a little tortoiseshell cat coming towards him. The cat asked, in friendly tones, "Where do you want to go, Hans?"

"I'm afraid you can't help me," said Hans.

"I know what you wish for," said the little cat. "You want a handsome horse. Come with me, serve me faithfully for seven years, and at the end of that time I will give you a finer horse than you have ever seen."

This is a strange cat, thought Hans, but I'll go with her and find out whether what she says is true. So he went away with the tortoiseshell cat to her enchanted castle. It was full of little cats who served her. They scampered nimbly up and down stairs in high spirits, amusing themselves. When they sat down to table in the evening, three of the cats made music. One played the double-bass, another the violin, and the third raised a trumpet to his mouth and blew out his cheeks out as he played. When they had eaten, the table was taken away and the tortoiseshell cat said, "Come along now, Hans, and dance with me!"

"No," he replied. "What, dance with a kitty-cat? I've never done such a thing in my life."

"Well, take him to bed, then," said the little cat to her cat servants. One of them carried a light to his bedroom, one took off his shoes, one his stockings, and finally one of them blew out the candle. Next morning they came back and helped him out of bed. One of them put his stockings on for him, another tied his garters, another fetched his shoes, yet another washed him, and finally one of the cats dried his face with her tail. This is certainly a comfortable place to live, said Hans to himself, and he was very happy with his new position.

However, he also had to work for the cat, and chop wood for her every day. She gave him a silver axe for the work, as well as a silver wedge and a silver saw, and a mallet made of copper. He worked hard, and lived in the cat's enchanted castle, where he was given good food and drink, but he never saw anyone apart from the tortoiseshell cat and the other cats in her household.

One day she told him, "Go and mow my meadow, and spread the grass out to dry." She gave him a silver scythe and a whetstone made of gold, and told him to bring everything back.

Hans went and did as she told him. When the work was done, he carried the scythe, the whetstone and the hay he had made home, and asked the cat whether she wouldn't give him his reward, for the seven years were up now.

"No," said the cat. "I have one more thing that you must do for me first. Here's building material of silver, a carpenter's hatchet, an angle iron and everything else you'll need, all made of silver. I want you to build me a little house."

So Hans built the cat a pretty little house. When he had finished it, he said now he had done all she asked, but he still didn't have a horse.

"Would you like to see my horses?" asked the cat.

"Yes, to be sure," said Hans. Then the cat opened the door of the little house – and there stood twelve proud horses, with coats so smooth and shining that you could see your reflection in them. Hans felt his heart leap at the sight. Now the little cat gave him food and drink again, and then she said, "Go home. I am not giving you the horse to take with you, but I will come myself and bring it to you in three days' time."

So Hans set off, and the cat showed him the way to the mill. But she hadn't even

given him new clothes to wear, so he had to go in the old, ragged smock that he had worn when he arrived, and after seven years it was far too short for him.

When he came home to the mill, the other miller's boys were back as well. Each of them had brought a horse with him, but one of the horses was blind and the other lame. "Well, Hans," they asked. "Where's your horse, then?"

"It will be coming in three days' time," said Hans.

At that they laughed and said, "Why, Hans, you simpleton, where would you get a horse? What a joke!"

Hans went into the mill, but the miller said he was not to sit down at the table with them; they'd be ashamed of a companion in such a torn and ragged smock. So they gave him a little food to take out of doors, and when they were going to bed in the evening the two others wouldn't let him have a bed himself. He had to crawl into the goose pen and lie down on hard straw.

When he awoke, the three days were over, and a coach drove up drawn by six horses whose coats shone wonderfully. A servant was leading a seventh horse, and that horse was for Hans the poor miller's boy.

But a king's beautiful daughter stepped out of the coach. She was none other than the little tortoiseshell cat whom poor Hans had served for seven years. She went into the mill and asked the miller where Hans, the smallest and youngest of his boys, might be.

"Oh, we can't let him into the parlor here," said the miller. "He's such a tattered, ragged sight that he has to sleep in the goose pen!"

The king's daughter said he was to be fetched at once. So they went to fetch him, and he came before the king's daughter in his shabby old smock. Then the servants who had come too unpacked magnificent clothes, Hans had to wash himself and put them on, and when he had done so no king could have looked more handsome. Then the lovely girl asked to see the horses that the other miller's boys had brought home. But one was blind and the other was lame. She told her grooms to bring in the seventh horse. When the miller saw it, he cried, "My word, a horse like that has never been seen in my yard before!"

"It is for Hans," said the king's daughter.

"If that is so," said the miller, "then he must have the mill."

But the king's daughter said the miller was to keep his mill. And she took her

faithful Hans by the hand, sat down with him in the coach, and drove away with him.

First they drove to the little house that he had built with silver tools. It had turned into a large castle, with everything inside and out made of gold and silver. Then they were married, and Hans was rich, so rich that he had enough to live on all his life. So let no one say that a man who seems to be a simpleton can never amount to anything.

HANS MY HEDGEHOG

There was once a farmer who had a great deal of money and property, but rich as he was one thing made him unhappy: he and his wife had no children. When he went into town with the other farmers, they often mocked him and asked why he had never had a child. That made him angry, and when he came home he said, "I wish I had a child, even if it were to be a hedgehog!" Then his wife did have a baby who was a hedgehog above the waist and a boy from the waist down, and when she saw the child she was horrified and told her husband, "Look at that! You've brought a curse down on us!"

The farmer said, "There's nothing we can do about it, and the boy must be baptised, but we can hardly ask anyone to stand godfather to him."

"We can only have him baptised as Hans my Hedgehog," said his wife.

When he was baptised, the priest said, "He can't sleep in an ordinary bed with all those prickly spines." A little straw was put behind the stove, and Hans my Hedgehog lay on it. His mother couldn't suckle him either, because his prickles would have hurt her. So he lay behind the stove for eight years, and his father was tired of him and wished he would die, but he didn't die, he just lay there.

Now one day there was a market in town, and the farmer said he would go. He asked his wife what she would like him to bring her. "A little meat and a few bread rolls, something for the household," she said. Then he asked the maidservant, who wanted a pair of slippers and a pair of stockings. Last of all he asked, "Hans my Hedgehog, what would you like me to bring you?" "Father," he said, "bring me a set of bagpipes!" When the farmer came home again, he gave his wife the meat and the rolls he had bought her, then he gave the maid her slippers and stockings, and last of all he went behind the stove and gave Hans my Hedgehog his bagpipes.

Once Hans my Hedgehog had the bagpipes, he said, "Father, go to the blacksmith and get him to shoe my rooster, and then I'll ride away and never come back again."

The farmer was glad to think of being rid of him, so he had the rooster shod, and when that was done Hans my Hedgehog sat on the rooster, rode away, and took some pigs and donkeys with him. He was planning to herd them out in the forest. Once in the forest, however, the rooster flew up to the top of a tall tree with him, and he sat there herding the donkeys and the swine for many long years, until the herd had grown very large, while his father knew nothing about him. But as he sat in the tree he played his bagpipes, and the music he made was very beautiful.

One day a king came riding by. He had lost his way in the forest, and heard the music. It surprised him, and he sent his servant to find out where the music was coming from. The servant looked, but all he could see was a small animal sitting up in a tree. It looked like a rooster with a hedgehog sitting on it, and the hedgehog was playing the music. Then the king told his servant to ask why the hedgehog was sitting there, and whether he knew the way back to his kingdom. At that Hans my Hedgehog climbed down from the tree and said he would show him the way, if the king would promise solemnly to give him whatever first came to meet him when he got home to the royal court, and he must put it in writing. Well, thought the king, I can promise that easily enough. I can write what I like, and Hans my Hedgehog won't understand it. So the king took pen and ink and wrote something down, and when he had done that Hans my Hedgehog showed him the way, and he arrived home safe and sound.

But his daughter, on seeing him in the distance, was so delighted that she ran to meet him and welcome him with a kiss. The king thought of Hans my Hedgehog, and told her what had happened to him, and how he had been obliged to promise a strange animal whatever first met him first at home; he had had to put it in writing as well. And the creature had been sitting on a rooster as if it were a horse, playing wonderful music. However, said the king, since the creature couldn't read he had written that Hans my Hedgehog was not to have whatever first met him. The princess was glad of that and said it was a good thing, because she would never have gone to such a creature.

Hans my Hedgehog went on herding the donkeys and the pigs, and he was always merry, sitting up in the tree and playing his bagpipes. Now it happened that another king came riding by with his servants and messengers. He had lost his way, and didn't know how to get home because the forest was so large. He too heard the beautiful music from far away and wondered what it was, telling a messenger to go and see. So the messenger found himself under the tree, and saw the rooster sitting there with Hans my Hedgehog on his back. The messenger asked what he was doing up there.

"Herding my donkeys and my pigs. But what do you want?"

The messenger said they had lost their way, and couldn't get back to their own kingdom; could he by any chance tell them the way to it? Then Hans my Hedgehog climbed down the tree and told the old king that he would show him the way if he promised to give him whatever first met him outside his royal castle as his own. The king said yes – and wrote down that Hans my Hedgehog should have it. When that

was done, Hans my Hedgehog rode ahead of the king on the rooster and showed him the way back to his kingdom.

When the king rode into the courtyard there was great rejoicing. He had an only daughter, who was very beautiful and she ran to meet him, flung her arms around him and kissed him, because she was so glad to see her old father back. She asked him where he had been so long, and he told her that he had lost his way and very nearly never came back at all, but when he was riding through a great forest a creature that was half hedgehog, half human, sitting astride a rooster in a tall tree, had helped him and shown him the way. But he had promised in return that the creature should have whatever first met him when he came back to the royal court, and it had been his daughter, so now he regretted it deeply. However, his daughter promised that she would gladly go with the creature when he came, for love of her old father.

Hans my Hedgehog went on herding his pigs, and the pigs had piglets until there were so many that the forest was full of them. Then Hans my Hedgehog didn't want to stay in the forest any longer, and he sent a message to his father saying they must clear out all the stables and sheds in the village, because he was coming back with such a huge herd of pigs that anyone who wanted could slaughter one. His father was upset to hear this, because he thought Hans my Hedgehog would have died long ago. However, Hans my Hedgehog mounted his rooster, drove the pigs ahead of him into the village and had them slaughtered. What a scene of butchery that was! You could hear the noise of it two hours' ride away. After that Hans my Hedgehog said, "Father, get the smith to shoe my rooster again, and then I will ride away and never come back."

Hans my Hedgehog rode away to the first kingdom, where the king had given orders that if someone came riding a rooster and carrying a set of bagpipes, they were all to shoot, at him, hack him and strike him down, to keep him from coming into the castle. When Hans my Hedgehog came riding up they fixed their bayonets and made for him, but he spurred on the rooster, who flew up into the air and over the gate, and came down outside the king's window. Hans my Hedgehog called to the king, asking him to make good his promise, or he and his daughter would lose their lives. The king spoke words of comfort to his daughter, asking her to go out to the creature to save both their lives. So she dressed herself in white, and her father gave her a carriage with six horses and magnificently dressed servants, along with money and property. She sat in the carriage, and Hans my Hedgehog with his rooster and his bagpipes sat beside her.

Then they said goodbye, and drove away, and the king thought he would never see them again. However, it didn't turn out like that, for when they were a little way outside the town, Hans my Hedgehog took the beautiful clothes off the king's daughter and pricked her with his hedgehog spines until she bled. "That's what you get for playing me false," he said. "Away with you, I don't want you." And he chased her away home, and no one had a good word for her all the rest of her days.

However, Hans my Hedgehog mounted his rooster and rode on with his bagpipes to the second kingdom, whose king he had also helped to find the way home. This second king had given orders that if someone looking like Hans my Hedgehog came along, his guards were to present arms in a salute, let him in with loud cheers, and take him to the king's castle. When the king's daughter saw him she was startled, because he looked so strange, but she thought there was nothing for it, she had given her father her word. So she welcomed Hans my Hedgehog, and they were married. He had to sit at the royal table, and she sat down at his side, and they ate and drank. When evening came, and they were going to bed, she was afraid of his spines. But he told her to have no fear, no harm would come to her, and he told the old king to station four men outside the bedchamber, and to light a great fire. When he went into the bedchamber and was going to lie down in bed, he said, he would slip out of his hedgehog skin and leave it on the floor beside the bed. Then the men must run in and throw it in the fire, and wait until the flames had consumed it entirely. When the clock struck eleven, he went into the bedchamber, stripped off his hedgehog skin, and left it beside the bed. Then the men came in, seized it swiftly and threw it on the fire, and when the fire had consumed it he was released, and lay in bed as a normal man, but charred black as if by burning. The king sent for his physician, who washed him with good salves and rubbed balm into him, his skin was made clean, and now he was a handsome young gentleman. When the king's daughter saw that, she was glad, and next morning they rose joyfully, ate and drank, and now their wedding was really celebrated. The old king handed the kingdom over to Hans my Hedgehog.

After several years, he and his wife went to see his father, and he told the old farmer that he was his son. His father said he had no son, he had had only one child who came into the world with the spines of a hedgehog and had gone away to seek his fortune. Then the young king revealed his identity, and his old father rejoiced and went back to his kingdom with him.

THE CHILDREN OF HAMELIN

In the year 1284 a man of very strange appearance was seen in the town of Hamelin. He wore a coat made of cloth of different colors, and he said that he was a rat-catcher. In return for a certain sum of money, he told the citizens, he could promise to rid the town of the many rats and mice that plagued it. The townspeople came to an agreement with him, and assured him that he would be paid a proper fee. At that the rat-catcher took out a little pipe and played music on it. The rats and mice immediately came scurrying out of all the houses and gathered around him. When he thought there were none left in the town he went out of Hamelin, followed by all the rats and mice. He led them down to the river Weser, where he hitched up his clothes and waded into the water, whereupon all the vermin followed him, fell into the river, and were drowned.

However, once the people of Hamelin were rid of their plague of rats and mice, they regretted promising the man a fee, and kept refusing to pay it on one pretext or another, so that in the end he went away angry and embittered. He came back on June the 26th, the feast day of St. John and St. Paul, at seven in the morning, or according to some versions of the story at mid-day, this time in the form of a huntsman with a fearsome face, wearing a strange red hat, and he began playing his pipe in the streets. This time, out came not rats and mice but children, great numbers of boys and girls four years old and over, including the mayor's grown-up daughter. The whole crowd followed the Piper, and he led them out to a mountain, into which he disappeared with them.

A nursemaid who had been carrying a baby and following the procession at a distance saw what happened, and she turned round and brought the news back to town. The parents of the boys and girls all ran out of doors, searching for their children in great distress, and the mothers set up a pitiful weeping and wailing. From then on, messengers were sent by land and water to all the places round about, asking whether the children of Hamelin, or even just some of them, had been seen there, but in vain. In all, a hundred and thirty children had been lost.

Some people say that two children who had been lagging behind came home, but one of them was blind and the other a deaf mute, so that the blind child could not show anyone the place where the children had disappeared, although he could tell the tale of how they had followed the piper, while the deaf mute could point to the place but had heard nothing. One little boy had run after the rest of them in his shirt, but

turned back to fetch his coat, and so he had escaped the fate of the rest, for when he returned to join them they had disappeared into an opening in a hill that is still pointed out today.

The street along which the children went out of the town gate was known until the middle of the 18th century (and probably to this day) as Silent Street, because no one was allowed to dance or play stringed instruments there. If a bride was being escorted to church for her wedding with music, the musicians had to fall silent while they were in that street. The mountain near Hamelin where the children disappeared is called the Poppenberg (or sometimes Koppenberg) and two stones in the form of a cross have been set up to right and left of it. Some say that the children were led into a cave and came out in Transylvania.

The following titles were illustrated by Lisbeth Zwerger, and have appeared in Michael Neugebauer Editions:

HANS CHRISTIAN ANDERSEN'S FAIRY TALES
THE LITTLE MERMAID · H.C. Andersen
THE LITTLE MERMAID · H.C. Andersen, MINI-MINEDITION
THE NIGHT BEFORE CHRISTMAS · Clement Clarke Moore
THE BREMEN TOWN MUSICIANS · The Brothers Grimm
NOAH'S ARK · Heinz Janisch
THE SWINEHERD · Hans Christian Andersen
THE PIED PIPER OF HAMELIN · The Brothers Grimm
THE SELFISH GIANT · Oscar Wilde, MINI-MINEDITION
LISBETH ZWERGER · THE WORLD OF IMAGINATION

Learn more about Lisbeth Zwerger and her books at:
www.minedition.com